Contents

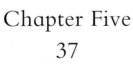

Chapter One

It was the first day of the school
holidays and there were lots of exciting
things Steve could have been doing.
He could have been skateboarding,
tree climbing or playing football.
But he wasn't doing any of them.

Instead he was stuck inside his dad's
dusty old chemist shop.

"I'm so bored!" he moaned.

"We haven't had a single customer
all day."

"Well, look on the bright side," said Dad cheerfully. "It means we've plenty of time for our annual spring clean." And with that he climbed his ladder to dust the top shelves.

Steve sighed. There had to be easier
ways to earn his pocket money.
Just then the bell above the shop
door rang.

A customer. At last! thought Steve.
It was an old woman dressed in black
wearing a pointy hat.

She looked like she was going to a
fancy dress party – as a witch!

"Warts!" growled the old woman.

"Pardon?" said Steve.

"Warts! I've got warts!"

She certainly did. They were all over
her nose.

Steve was wondering what she wanted
him to do about them, when Dad
called down from the ladder,
"Wart Cream. Third shelf on the left."
Steve found it and put it in a bag.

"And shampoo!" barked the woman.
"I need shampoo for people with very
greasy hair."

She certainly did. Her long black hair
was greasy enough to fry chips in!
"The green bottle at the back," said
Dad cheerfully.
"And I want lipstick, too!" ordered the
woman. "Black lipstick!"
"Bottom shelf, next to the green
eyeshadow," called Dad.

Steve found it and took the old woman's money.

She winked at Steve and shuffled off, muttering to herself about finding a shop that sold snail snot!

Snail snot? thought Steve.

Chapter Two

Steve wanted to ask his dad what snail snot was used for, but the bell above the door rang again.

It was another customer!

Except there wasn't anyone there.

That's odd, thought Steve.
Just then he felt a nip on
his ear.
"Yikes," he yowled.
Then he heard a
flutter of wings.
"Dad! I think there's a bird in the shop."

Dad was still up his
ladder. "Mmm, it's
probably just a bat."

14

"Yes," said a voice. "Just a bat."

The voice belonged to a wizened old man wearing a shiny black cape who had suddenly appeared from nowhere.

"Plasters – I need an extra-big box,"
said the old man softly.

"Next to the soap," called Dad from
the top of his ladder.

"And I need toothpaste. Lots of toothpaste," he told Steve with a grin, revealing two long, sharp, pointy teeth.

Yikes, thought Steve.

The man looked rather like a vampire.

"And stain remover," said the old man. "I have some troublesome blood stains that won't come out."
Steve shivered.

But he knew where the toothpaste and the stain remover were.
The man paid Steve for them.

Then suddenly Steve understood.

The fancy dress party!

He was obviously going to the same
one as the witch.

Steve smiled at the man.

"I like your costume."

The old man winked at Steve and then
suddenly vanished.

Chapter Three

"Pass up those tissues," said Steve's dad from the top of his ladder.

Steve got the tissues. "I can't reach!"

"Perhaps I can help?"

Steve turned to see the biggest and hairiest man he'd ever seen.

Actually, he looked more like a wolf
than a man.

As the man passed the tissues up
to Dad, Steve had a good long
look at him.

He had hair everywhere.

It sprouted from his cuffs,

the neck of

his shirt

and even out

of his ears.

"I need some nail clippers,"
said the man in a deep,
growly voice.

He certainly did. His nails looked like
claws – long, pointy and very dirty.

"Next to the nail varnish," called down Dad.

Steve swallowed hard. The hairy man had a tail!

"And an extra-strong comb!"

"Over by the shampoo," said Dad.

Of course! He was going to the same fancy dress party as the witch and the vampire.

He was supposed to be a werewolf!

"You really do look like one, you know," said Steve when he took the man's money.

TRIAL PRICE!

15

The man winked at him and then
trotted out of the shop.

Chapter Four

I wish I could go to a fancy dress party, thought Steve. *It would be much better than being stuck in this boring old shop.* Just then there was a thundering sound outside.

"Dad, I think there's a storm coming."

"Mmm, maybe," said his dad.

"Or maybe it's just a horse."

Steve peered out of the shop window.

It was a horse.

But not like any horse Steve had ever

seen before.

Big and black, it had wild eyes and
steam coming out of its nostrils.
Its rider swung himself out of the
saddle and flung open the shop door.
Steve was nearly knocked over
by the gust of wind that came
with him.

The man was tall and thin and
shrouded in black.

Steve couldn't even see his face.

"Throat sweets," he gasped from under his hood.

"Second aisle," called Dad from the top of his ladder.

"Extra-strong," gasped the voice.

Steve still couldn't see his head.

And then he did.

It was tucked under the man's arm!

"ARRRRGH!" yelled Steve.

He was so surprised he dropped

the throat sweets.

But then he guessed.

"Of course," he said. "You must

be the headless horseman. You're

going to the fancy dress party, too!"

The head smirked, but said nothing.

"I love your costume. How do you do

that thing with your head?"

asked Steve.

"Let me show you," rasped

the head.

He pulled back his hood and
revealed . . .

Nothing!

There was no head there, just a
stumpy neck.

"ARRRRGH!" screamed Steve.

Chapter Five

The headless horseman's head winked
at Steve from under his arm and then
he turned and left the shop, clutching
his throat sweets.

"I hope he paid for them," said Dad
from the top of his ladder.

Steve was stunned.

"Dad, that man didn't have a head!

Well, at least not attached to his body!"

"As I always tell you, Steve," said his dad, climbing down from his ladder. "There's always someone worse off than you."

Steve could see his point.

Suddenly, he had a thought. If the headless horseman *was* real, then the others might be, too.

Perhaps the old woman *was* a witch.

Maybe the old man *was* a vampire.

And the hairy wolf man might
actually *be* a real werewolf.

Steve felt his knees begin to knock.

"Right then, that's me done," said his

dad. "You can go off and play now if

you like."

"Play?" said Steve. "I don't want to go

off and play!"

"Ah!" said Dad. "So, working here

isn't as boring as you thought?"

"Boring?" said Steve. "No way!"

He was about to
tell his dad all about
the creepy customers
he'd served, when
he noticed his dad
was grinning.
"You know Steve,
there's never a dull
moment when you're
a shopkeeper! You
never know who . . .
or rather, what . . .
your next customer
might be!"

He gave Steve an extra-big wink and
went behind the counter, chuckling
softly to himself.

About the Author and Illustrator

Samantha Hay comes from Scotland. For the past ten years she has worked in television, but she is currently

taking time out to look after her wee girl and write stories. *Creepy Customers* is her first book to be published. "My big brother always tells me I look a bit like a vampire," says Sam. "My skin is quite white, and I love red lipstick! So fancy dress parties aren't a problem for me!"

Sarah Warburton was born in North Wales but now lives in Bristol with her husband. She has been illustrating books for over ten years. Sarah says, "As a girl I would always go to Halloween parties as a witch. However, I don't think I'd enjoy being a real witch as I'm terrified of spiders and allergic to cats! Witches are great fun to draw, though, as they're mostly ugly, mean and warty!"

Tips for Beginner Readers

1. Think about the cover and the title of the book. What do you think it will be about? While you are reading, think about what might happen next and why.

2. As you read, ask yourself if what you're reading makes sense. If it doesn't, try rereading or look at the pictures for clues.

3. If there is a word that you do not know, look carefully at the letters, sounds, and word parts that you do know. Blend the sounds to read the word. Is this a word you know? Does it make sense in the sentence?

4. Think about the characters, where the story takes place, and the problems the characters in the story faced. What are the important ideas in the beginning, middle and end of the story?

5. Ask yourself questions like:
    Did you like the story?
    Why or why not?
    How did the author make it fun to read?
    How well did you understand it?

Maybe you can understand the story better if you read it again!